THE CABIN

THAT
MOOSE
BUILT

Chérie B. Stihler
Illustrated by Jeremiah Trammell

Friends are Treasures!

PAWS IV *published by* SASQUATCH BOOKS

For homebuilders everywhere...
For Scott, with all my love—Chérie

Printed in China
Published by Sasquatch Books
Distributed by Publishers Group West
12 11 10 09 08 07   9 8 7 6 5 4 3 2

Interior design: Stewart A. Williams
Interior composition: Bob Suh

Library of Congress Cataloging-in-Publication
Data is available.

ISBN: 1-57061-446-6

More about the author at www.cheriestihler.com.

Sasquatch Books
119 South Main Street, Suite 400
Seattle, WA 98104
(206) 467-4300
www.sasquatchbooks.com
custserv@sasquatchbooks.com

Lakes still have their ice on top—but it's time to turn the **SOD.**
The cabin will get started when the ground is almost **THAWED.**

Green shoots peek through snowdrifts, time is growing near.
The fireweed will tell us when the building season's here.

EVERYONE
must help out—
not a moment can be lost!
Summer is the time
to BUILD
before the winter frost.

This is the cabin
that Moose built.

These are the shingles that **LEAK** and **SQUEAK**

on the roof with the patches that valley and peak

on top of the cabin that Moose built.

These are the floorboards that **GROAN** and **CREAK**

under the shingles that leak and squeak

on top of the cabin that Moose built.

Days start to grow longer
and stems stretch up **HIGH,**

Alaska's Midnight Sun dances
slowly in the **SKY.**

Hammer, hammer, hammer—
there is much to do,
my friend.
Winter may seem far away
but it will come again.

These are the walls with
wires **INSIDE** and
fresh coats of paint,
now almost **DRIED**

that rest on the
floorboards that
groan and creak
under the shingles that
leak and squeak

on top of the cabin
that Moose built.

These are the pipes that jiggle and **SLIDE** behind the walls with the wires **INSIDE**

that rest on the floorboards that groan and creak under the shingles that leak and squeak

on top of the cabin that Moose built.

Summer's half over, will the cabin be **READY?**

Days are now shorter but the workload is **STEADY.**

Hammer, hammer, hammer—there is much to do, my FRIEND.
Winter will return and then our building time must END.

Here is the fireplace
all cracked and BUMPY
made with the mortar
all gooey and CLUMPY

bent by the pipes
that jiggle and slide
behind the walls
with the wires inside

that rest on the floorboards
that groan and creak
under the shingles
that leak and squeak

on top of the cabin
that Moose built.

This is the wallpaper
crooked and LUMPY
near the large fireplace
all cracked and BUMPY

bent by the pipes
that jiggle and slide
behind the walls
with the wires inside

that rest on the floorboards
that groan and creak
under the shingles
that leak and squeak

on top of the cabin that Moose built.

FIREWEED blossoms race to the top,
It is a reminder that SOON we must stop.

Hammer, hammer, hammer—there is much to do, my friend
Hints of winter wave at us. We must keep building 'til the end.

Here are the windows
that wobble and **BREAK.**
Work has to stop
while they fix the **MISTAKE**

on the wall with the paper
that's crooked and lumpy
near the large fireplace
all cracked and bumpy

bent by the pipes
that jiggle and slide
behind the walls
with the wires inside

that rest on the floorboards that groan and creak
under the shingles that leak and squeak

on top of the cabin that Moose built.

These are the doors that **WIGGLE** and shake
that made those two windows **WOBBLE** and break

on the wall with the paper
that's crooked and lumpy
near the large fireplace
all cracked and bumpy

bent by the pipes
that jiggle and slide
behind the walls
with the wires inside

that rest on the floorboards
that groan and creak
under the shingles
that leak and squeak

on top of the cabin that Moose built.

Leaves change their colors, geese fly overhead.
Soon the aurora will dance there instead.

Hammer, hammer, hammer—not a moment to be lost.
Autumn smells remind us that there is an evening frost.

This is the **ARMCHAIR** that's comfy and wide
with big **FLUFFY** pillows and ribbons just tied

beyond the red doors that wiggle and shake
that made those two windows wobble and break

on the wall with the paper
that's crooked and lumpy
near the large fireplace
all cracked and bumpy

bent by the pipes
that jiggle and slide
behind the walls
with the wires inside

that rest on the floorboards that groan and creak
under the shingles that leak and squeak

on top of the cabin that Moose built.

This is the **BOOKSHELF**
that **LEANS** to one side
next to the armchair
that's comfy and wide

beyond the red doors
that wiggle and shake
that made those two windows
wobble and break

on the wall with the paper
that's crooked and lumpy
near the large fireplace
all cracked and bumpy

bent by the pipes that jiggle and slide
behind the walls with the wires inside
that rest on the floorboards that groan and creak
under the shingles that leak and squeak

on top of the cabin that Moose built.

Fireweed blossoms
turn fluffy and
WHITE.
Alaska prepares
for a long winter
NIGHT.

Hammer,
hammer,
hammer—
but we must now
stop, my friend.

Winter has returned.
The building time
is at an end.

This is the lamp with the golden glow LIGHTS.
Moose can be cozy on dark winter NIGHTS.

It sits on the bookshelf that leans to one side
next to the armchair that's comfy and wide

beyond the red doors that wiggle and shake
that made those two windows wobble and break
on the wall with the paper that's crooked and lumpy
near the large fireplace all cracked and bumpy

bent by the pipes that jiggle and slide
behind the walls with the wires inside
that rest on the floorboards that groan and creak
under the shingles that leak and squeak

on top of the cabin that Moose built.

SURPRISE!

These are the pals Moose is proud to call **FRIENDS!**
They finish the cabin just as summer **ENDS.**

They hammered for many long days and **NIGHTS!**
They wired the lamp with the golden glow **LIGHTS.**

They built the big bookshelf that leans to one side.
They covered the armchair that's comfy and wide.

They fixed the red doors
that wiggle and **SHAKE.**

They taped up the windows
that wobble and **BREAK.**

They smoothed out the wallpaper, crooked and lumpy.
They built the stone fireplace all cracked and bumpy.

They tied down the pipes that jiggle and **SLIDE.**
They strung line in the walls with the wires **INSIDE.**

They nailed down the floorboards that groan and creak.
They patched all the shingles that leak and squeak.

They helped with **THE CABIN THAT MOOSE BUILT.**

Old Porcupine's Housewarming Brownies

Ingredients:

¼ cup brown sugar
¾ cup granulated sugar
½ cup (1 stick) unsalted butter, softened
2 eggs
1 teaspoon vanilla
½ cup cocoa powder
½ cup all-purpose flour
1 cup fresh cranberries

Directions:

Preheat oven to 350 degrees F.
Butter 10-inch round baking dish.

In a large mixing bowl, beat the sugars with the butter. Add eggs and vanilla and beat again to mix well. Then add the cocoa powder and stir until blended. Gently stir in flour just until ingredients combine. Do not over mix. Finally, stir in cranberries and pour batter into the buttered baking dish.

Bake until brownies pull away from the edge of dish, about 20 to 25 minutes. Allow brownie pan to cool and then cut into wedges.

SERVES EIGHT